Charlotte County Library
3 0000 00042 7587

W9-DBQ-775

SURFING

BY RAY McCLELLAN

TORQUE™

BELLWETHER MEDIA • MINNEAPOLIS, MN

TORQUE™

Are you ready to take it to the extreme? Torque books thrust you into the action-packed world of sports, vehicles, and adventure. These books may include dirt, smoke, fire, and dangerous stunts.
WARNING: Read at your own risk.

This edition first published in 2008 by Bellwether Media.

Library of Congress Cataloging-in-Publication Data
McClellan, Ray.
Surfing / by Ray McClellan.
p. cm. — (Torque : action sports)
Summary: "Amazing photography accompanies engaging information about surfing. The combination of high-interest subject matter and light text is intended for students in grades 3 through 7"—Provided by publisher.
Includes bibliographical references and index.
ISBN-13: 978-1-60014-145-4 (hardcover : alk. paper)
ISBN-10: 1-60014-145-5 (hardcover : alk. paper)
1. Surfing—Juvenile literature. I. Title.

GV839.55.M33 2008
797.3'2—dc22 2007040559

CONTENTS

WHAT IS SURFING?

Ocean waves can have incredible power. Waves often build in strength and size as they move toward shore. Surfing is the sport of riding waves. Most surfers stand on boards while they ride. Beginners can **body surf** without standing up or even using a board. Surfing **professionals** take on the most powerful and dangerous waves. Some even launch themselves into the air to do daring tricks while they surf.

Surfing is one of the oldest action sports. Most people believe the sport started on the Hawaiian Islands.

The crew of a British ship wrote about the sport in 1779 when they stopped at the islands. They saw native Hawaiians riding waves while standing on long wooden boards.

EQUIPMENT

Surfers today can choose from a variety of boards. The two main types are **shortboards** and **longboards**. A shortboard measures about 6 to 7 feet (2 meters) long. Its small size makes it easy to control. Shortboards are great for doing tricks. Longboards measure 9 feet (3 meters) or longer. They are more stable than shortboards. Surfers can balance more easily on longboards.

RIP CURL

Surfers need only a few other pieces of equipment. A **leash** wraps around a surfer's ankle and connects to the board. It keeps the board from floating away if the surfer wipes out. Some surfers add a special **wax** to their board for a smoother ride. Some wear **wetsuits** to keep warm in areas where the water is very cold.

ROXY

SURFING IN ACTION

There are several key steps to riding a wave. Surfers paddle their boards 200 feet (60 meters) or more away from shore to watch for a big wave. Every wave is different. Some are bigger and better for surfing than others.

When surfers see a good wave coming, they start paddling hard toward shore. They need to build up speed before they can stand up on their boards.

They stand up when the wave is just starting to **break** behind them. The biggest waves create a **tube**. Surfers can ride inside of it. They cut back and forth under the **crest** to keep balance. They can also launch tricks as they speed along. A ride ends when a surfer jumps off the board or wipes out.

Competitions let the top surfers show off their skills. The best of the best compete on the World Championship Tour. Judges score each surfer's ride. They look at tricks, wave size, and the length of the ride.

Fast Fact

Funboards combine features of shortboards and longboards. They're good for doing tricks. They are also stable and easy to learn on.

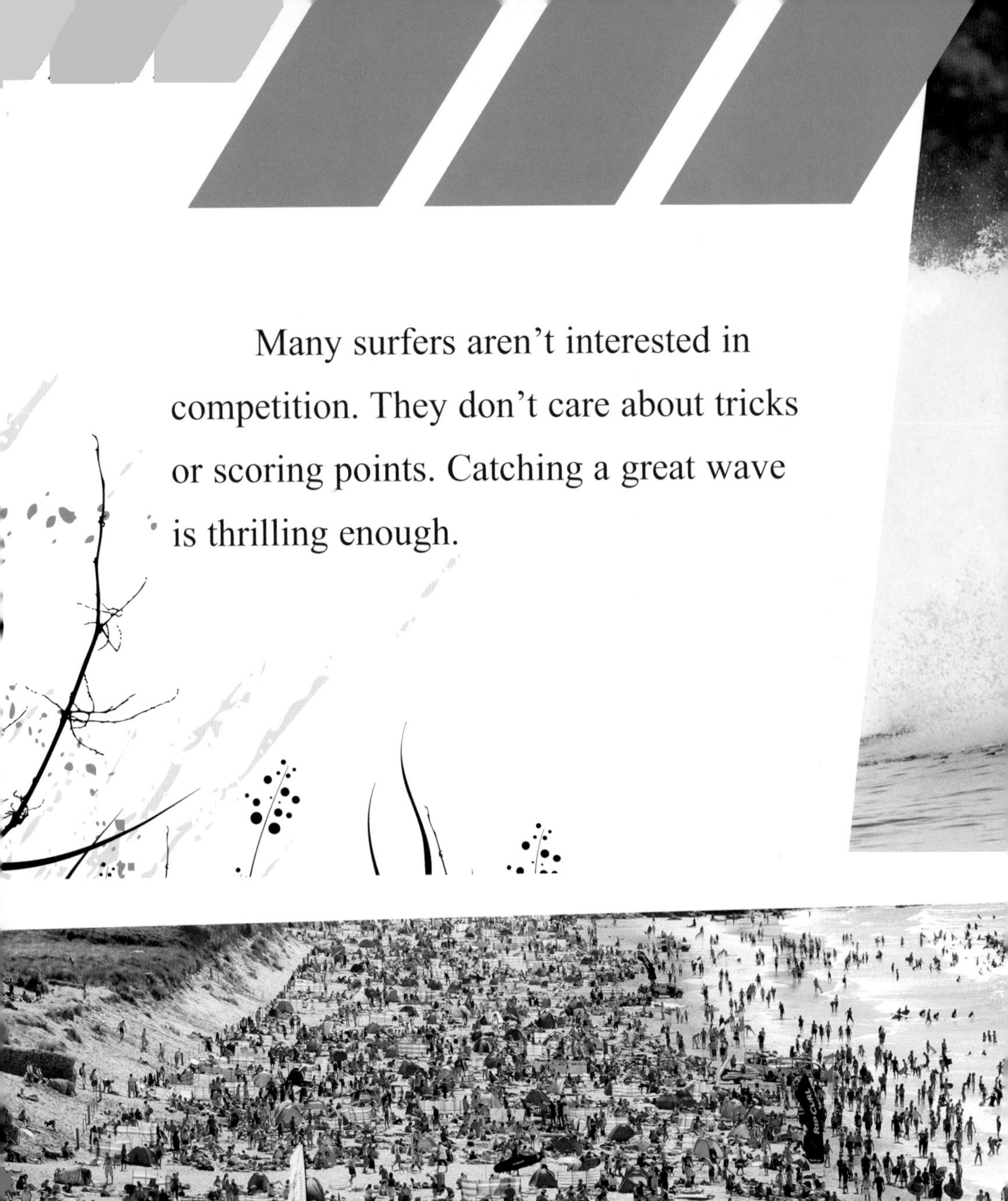

Many surfers aren't interested in competition. They don't care about tricks or scoring points. Catching a great wave is thrilling enough.

FAST FACT
Smart surfers never surf alone. Surfing with a friend is more fun and much safer.

For most people, surfing is simply about enjoying the excitement of the sport and power of the ocean.

GLOSSARY

body surf—to ride waves without using a board

break—to fall; a wave breaks when it approaches the shore or when it crashes into another wave moving in the opposite direction.

crest—the top edge of a breaking wave

leash—a strap that connects a surfer's ankle to the board

longboard—a long surfboard measuring about 9 feet (3 meters) or longer

professional—someone who is paid to compete in a sport

shortboard—a short surfboard measuring 6 to 7 feet (2 meters) or shorter

tube—the long, tunnel-like section under a breaking wave

wax—a material surfers put on their boards for a smoother ride

wetsuit—a waterproof body suit that keeps a surfer warm in cold water

TO LEARN MORE

AT THE LIBRARY

Bizley, Kirk. *Surfing*. Chicago, Ill.: Heinemann, 2000.

Crossingham, John. *Extreme Surfing*. New York: Crabtree, 2004.

Peterson, Christine. *Extreme Surfing*. Mankato, Minn.: Capstone, 2005.

ON THE WEB

Learning more about surfing is as easy as 1, 2, 3.

1. Go to www.factsurfer.com
2. Enter “surfing” into search box.
3. Click the “Surf” button and you will see a list of related web sites.

With factsurfer.com, finding more information is just a click away.

INDEX

The images in this book are reproduced through the courtesy of: AFP/Stringer/Getty Images, cover; Jonathan Wood/Stringer/Getty Images, pp. 3, 9 (right); Paul Kennedy/Getty Images, p. 5; Handout/Getty Images, pp. 6, 13, 15, 16-17, 19 (bottom); North Wind Picture Archives/Alamy, p. 7; Grant Ellis/Getty Images, p. 9 (left); Matt Cardy/Stringer/Getty Images, pp. 10, 18; Getty Images/Stringer, p. 11 (top); Karen Wilson/Handout/Getty Images, p. 11 (bottom); Pierre Tostee/Handout/Getty Images, p. 12; Jason Childs/Contributor/Getty Images, pp. 14, 19 (top); Ray Jarvis, p. 20; Gary Paul Lewis, p. 21.